Arachnid Attack!

School Specialty
Publishing
Columbus, Ohio

By Teresa Domnauer

School Specialty
Publishing

Copyright © 2007 School Specialty Publishing, a member
of the School Specialty Family.

Printed in the United States of America. All rights reserved. Except as permitted
under the United States Copyright Act, no part of this publication may be
reproduced or distributed in any form or by any means, or stored in a database or
retrieval system, without prior written permission from the publisher, unless
otherwise indicated.

Library of Congress Cataloging-in-Publication Data is on file with the publisher.

Send all inquiries to:
School Specialty Publishing
8720 Orion Place
Columbus, OH 43240-2111

ISBN 0-7696-6550-0

1 2 3 4 5 6 7 8 9 10 PHX 10 09 08 07

You might think a spider is an insect.
You might think a tick is an insect, too.
But they are not!
These creatures belong to
another animal family.
They are arachnids (uh RACK nidz).

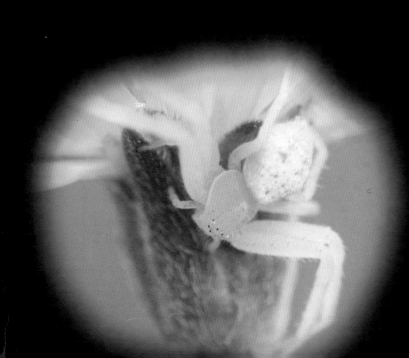

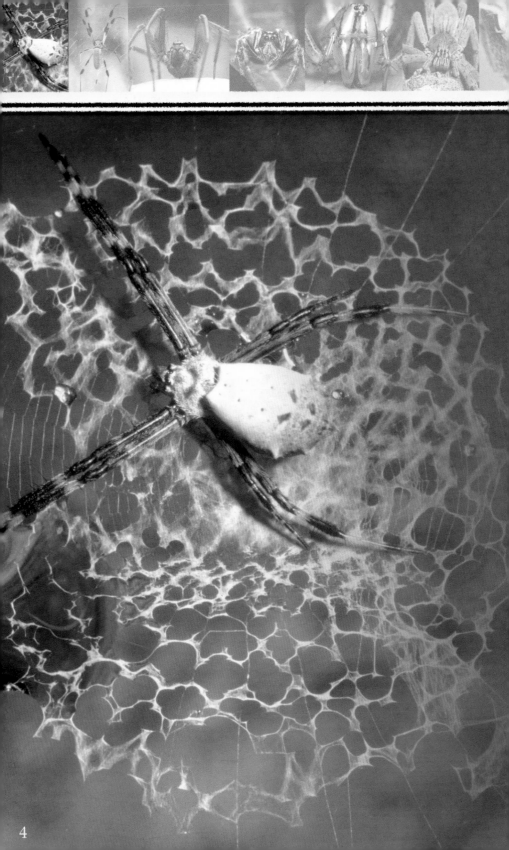

Orb Weaver Spider

What does this arachnid do?
It makes strings of silk.
Then, it spins the strings of silk
into a round web.
You might see a spider web like this
in your backyard.

Golden Silk Spider

What does this arachnid do?
It traps insects in its web.
The insects stick to the gooey silk.
They become food for the spider.

Wolf Spider

What does this arachnid do?
It hunts for food.
It bites its prey with sharp teeth.
These teeth are called *fangs*.

Jumping Spider

What does this arachnid do?
It sneaks up on insects.
Then, it jumps on them and eats them.
The jumping spider also jumps
away from danger.

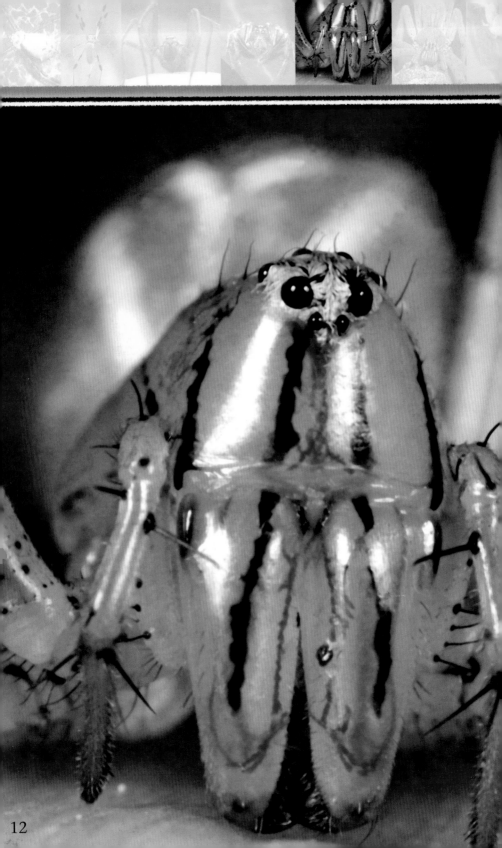

Lynx Spider

What does this arachnid do?
It runs quickly over plants and flowers.
The lynx spider chases insects.
Sometimes, it leaps out and
surprises them.

Huntsman Spider

What does this arachnid do?
It hides in trees.
Its brown color looks like tree bark.
This makes it hard for other animals
to see the huntsman spider.

Crab Spider

What does this arachnid do?
Sometimes, it changes color!
A crab spider hides in flowers.
It can change its color to blend in
with a flower's bright blooms.

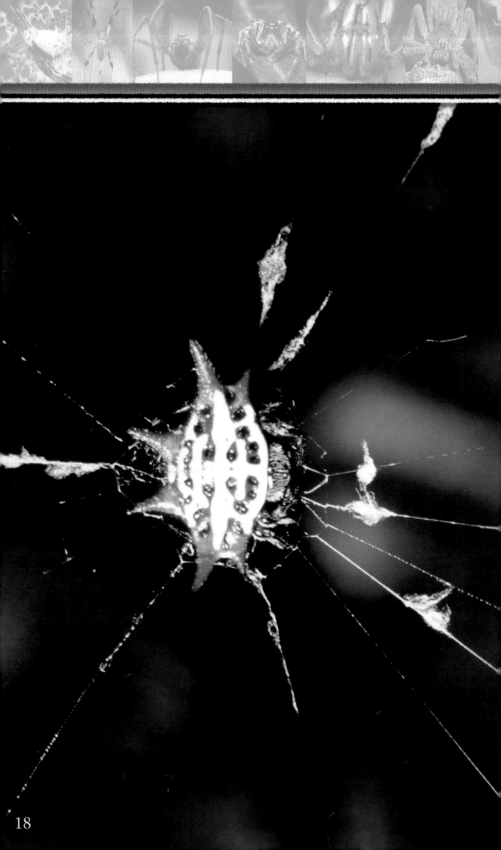

Jewel Spider

What does this arachnid do?
It keeps birds away.
Birds do not want to eat
the jewel spider.
It has pointy spines on its body!

Black Widow Spider

What does this arachnid do?
Sometimes, it bites.
Most spiders don't bite people.
But once in a while, the black
widow does.
Its bite can make a person very sick!

Tarantula

What does this arachnid do?
It grows and grows.
Tarantulas are the largest kinds
of spiders in the world.
Some are as big as your hand!

Grass Spider

What does this arachnid do?
It hides in its web.
It waits for an insect to crawl onto it.
Then, it runs quickly to catch it.

Daddy Longlegs

What does this arachnid do?
It crawls quickly.
A daddy longlegs has eight
long, thin legs.
It looks a lot like a spider,
but it is a different kind of arachnid.

Scorpion

What does this arachnid do?
It stings.
The scorpion has a sharp stinger
on the end of its tail.
It also has pointy claws
called *pincers* (PIN surz).

EXTREME FACTS ABOUT ARACHNID ATTACK!

- An orb weaver spider usually spins a new web every night.

- The silk of a golden silk spider is yellow. It shines like gold in the sunlight.

- The wolf spider got its name because it hunts and eats its prey just like a wolf does.

- The jumping spider has the best eyesight of all spiders.

- There are over 400 different kinds of lynx spiders.

- People often mistake the huntsman spider for a tarantula because of the spider's furry body.

- The crab spider can walk sideways and backward, just like a crab does at the beach.

- Sometimes, the jewel spider is called the "Christmas spider." That's because it can be found in great numbers around Christmastime in parts of Australia.

- A female black widow spider lays anywhere from 100 to 500 eggs at a time.

- Sometimes, a tarantula will catch its dinner, wrap it in its strings of silk, and save it for later to eat.

- The grass spider weaves a web that is shaped like a funnel.

- Daddy longlegs are also called "harvestman spiders."

- A mother scorpion carries her babies on her back.

- The bites of some ticks can make people and animals very sick.

Tick

What does this arachnid do?
It crawls onto another animal.
It bites the animal and drinks
its blood.
That is how the tick gets its food!